This book belongs to:

Meyer Vorpahl

Meyer —
We hope you will always
enjoy visiting us "in
the woods" in Door County!
We love you so....
Mema
&
Pepa

6/2024

Dedication:

To my beloved Grandma, Sally McBride, who is the love, light, and foundation of our family. Thank you for creating the sweetest childhood memories for me, the bond we share will always be incredibly special to me.

All my love to you!
Your Granddaughter, Corrin

Grandma's lessons for a happy life:
Have something to do
Have someone to love
Have something to look forward to

A Door County Story

Based on a true story.

written by Corrin Wendell

illustrated by Folksbfables
including Neethi Joseph, Indu Shaji, Vinay Jacob

In Door County's magic, Grandma in the Woods held a place,
Where summer days unfolded, memories to embrace.
Making the turn onto Highway 57, my heart would flutter,
Eighteen last miles seemed like eternity, so much to discover.

Midway down Bluff Road, her blue house appeared,
Nestled among trees, love and warmth were revealed.
The gravel driveway crackled, as I arrived with delight,
"Grandma in the Woods" read the sign, oh, what a sight!

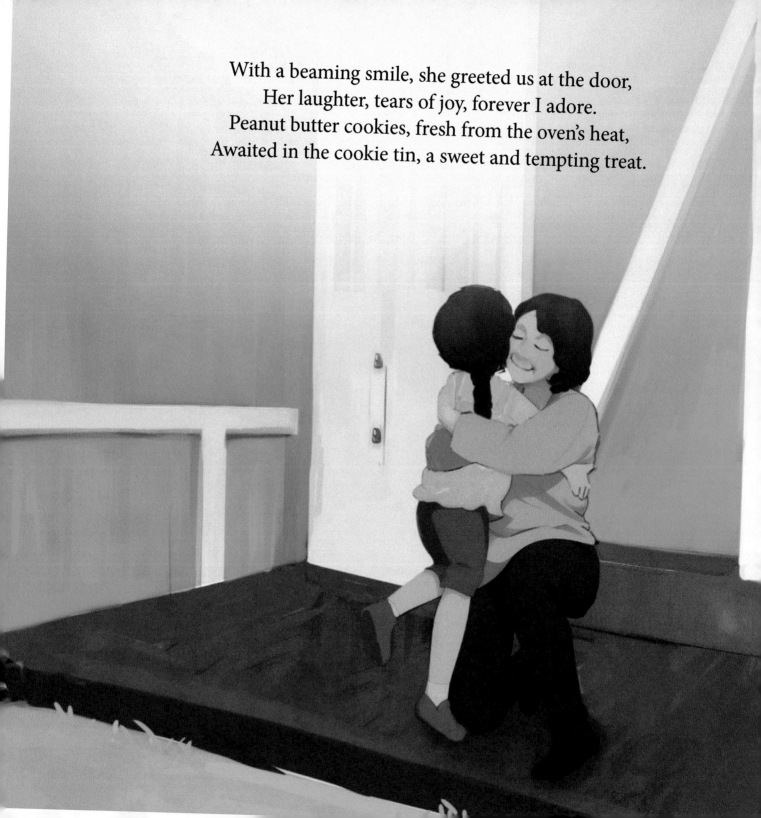

With a beaming smile, she greeted us at the door,
Her laughter, tears of joy, forever I adore.
Peanut butter cookies, fresh from the oven's heat,
Awaited in the cookie tin, a sweet and tempting treat.

Each day spent with Grandma, a Door County Day,
A slice of paradise, where worries would go away.
Mornings at her home, the sunlight painted the kitchen scene,
Pancakes on the flat top, fresh jam, brewing a cup of tea.

We embarked on drives, up the peninsula's way,
To Gills Rock, the winding road, where the ferry to Washington Island lay.
Schoolhouse Beach to swim in the crystal-clear sea,
Lunch at the Shoreline, cherries from Seaquist's tree.
The cherry blossoms fell gently, like confetti from above,
We'd sing our favorite Patsy Cline, so full of love.

Friday nights meant the Skyway Drive-In theatre, a magical escape,
Double features, popcorn, and Slo-Pokes, memories we'd make.
Playing on the merry-go-round, loud shrieks and cries,
Blankets to keep us warm, under the dark starlit skies.

In Grandma's Woods, time danced in a blissful haze,
Exploring moss-covered flagstones, our imaginations ablaze.
Chasing fireflies in La La Land, inhaling the forest's earthly scent,
Spending nights beneath stars, walkie-talkies in our tent.

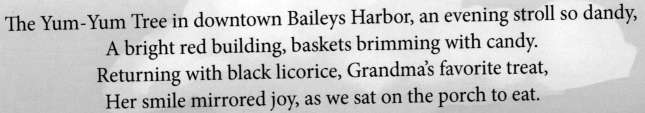

The Yum-Yum Tree in downtown Baileys Harbor, an evening stroll so dandy,
A bright red building, baskets brimming with candy.
Returning with black licorice, Grandma's favorite treat,
Her smile mirrored joy, as we sat on the porch to eat.

Warm Bay-side beach days, sand castles built with glee,
Waves crashing, seagulls diving, enjoying the lake's majesty.
Climbing Eagle Tower, with a beautiful view,
Nicolet Beach to Horseshoe Island, a sight for me and you.

Campfires at Grandma's, marshmallows on a stick,
Her childhood stories and songs, memories we'd pick.
With every S'more, a burst of summer's sweet embrace,
Forever chasing fireflies, leaving a smile on my face.

Wilson's in Ephraim, a jelly bean cone filled with delight,
Watching sunsets paint the sky, ice cream in the twilight.
A highlight of summer, a memory to hold,
A walk down to Anderson Dock, the beautiful graffiti unfolds.

Northern Sky Theatre, funny musicals under the trees,
Our laughter under the lights, a moment to seize.
Back at Grandma's games galore, laughter filling the air,
Dominoes, Scrabble, playing cards, the joy we all shared.

Downtown library visits, Grandma's love for the written word,
Picking out books, reading Anne of Green Gables, how absurd!
Baileys Harbor beach nights, swimming under the moon,
Grandma kept the towels warm, hot chocolate coming soon.

Al Johnson's goats on the grassy roof, a whimsical display,
Swedish pancakes and meatballs savored, Annika's generosity in every way.
Dirndls, clogs, and FIKA, a traveler's delight,
Like a charming Swedish village, a picturesque sight.

Jumping off the dock in Sister Bay, with waves as our cue,
Funny leaps into the water, a summertime debut.
The sunbeams dancing, casting their golden hour glow,
One last jump, look out below!

An early morning hike at Toft Point always called,
Leaves rustling beneath our feet, memories enthralled.
A stroll through the meadows out to the point, under the azure sky,
Inhaling trillium scents making our spirits fly.

Fish boils at the Old Post Office, smoke plumes reached the sky,
Stories around the crackling fire, the sweet treat of cherry pie.
Whitefish and potatoes simmered in the boiling pot,
We lingered in these moments in our favorite spot.

Listening to Grandma's tales, such cherished gems,
Filled with love and adventure, like a heartfelt anthem.
Sharing stories of her childhood, eyes full of laughter,
Always wisdom in her words, a storytelling master.

As the cool air of fall gently whispered in the woods,
We knew school beckoned, and Grandma understood.
For in Grandma's Woods, we find joy and are free,
A magical place where love and memories forever will be.

So we waved farewell, with promises in our hearts,
Knowing that Grandma's Woods would never truly depart.
With gratitude for the summer spent in her care,
We will always have these moments for us to share.

Until next time, dear Grandma Sally, we eagerly await,
The joyous reunion at your door, we won't be late.
For a Door County summer, spent in the Woods so grand,
Is etched in our souls, like the imprints on the sand.

With a heart full of love and a tearful goodbye,
So cherished and sweet, where time gently flies.
Her wisdom and warmth, like a comforting song,
We will return to Grandma's embrace, where we truly belong.

THE END

About the Author:

Corrin Wendell has held Door County dear to her heart and a second home for many decades. Since her grandparents retired to the peninsula in the 1980s, Corrin and her family have cherished frequent visits spanning over 40 years, including attending Gibraltar for a short time. Fond memories were woven during summers spent with her Grandma in Baileys Harbor, where Corrin and her sister Gretchen had incredible youthful adventures and often took up enjoyable summer jobs and made many life-long friends. Today, Corrin loves passing down these cherished recollections to her son Jack, who joins her in reliving those nostalgic moments. Whether gliding through the waters of Ephraim on a kayak or taking refreshing dips in Lake Michigan, Corrin finds immense joy in the beauty of Door County and plans to fulfil her dream of retiring there someday!

Corrin lives in Saint Paul, Minnesota, along with her husband Scott and their amazing son Jack. Corrin is also the author of "Ava Tanner, the City Planner." an Urban Planner, Founder and Executive Director of YEP! Youth Engagement Planning, a National and International Keynote Speaker, and named an International Women Planner of Influence.